MW00946261

Click!

JEFFREY EBBELER

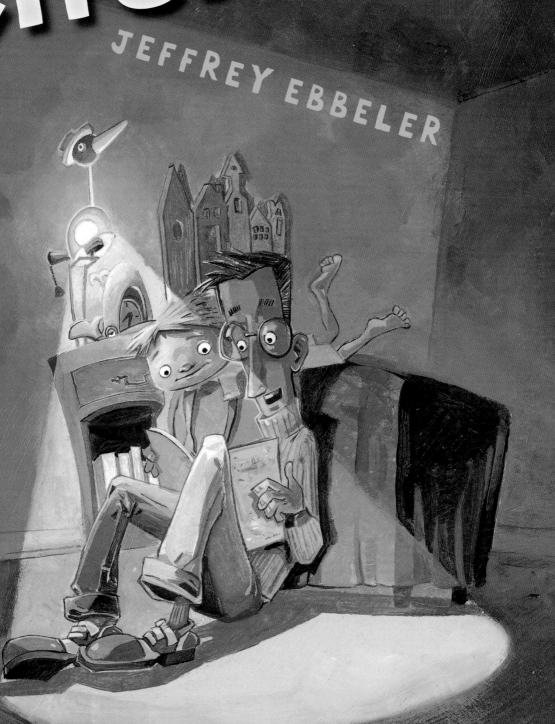

Holiday House / New York

For Eileen

HOLIDAY HOUSE is registered in the U.S. Patent and Trademark Office.

Printed and Bound in October 2014 at Toppan Leefung, DongGuan City, China.

The artwork was created with acrylic paint on paper.

www.holidayhouse.com

First Edition

1 3 5 7 9 10 8 6 4 2

Library of Congress Cataloging-in-Publication Data

Ebbeler, Jeffrey, author, illustrator.

Click! / by Jeffrey Ebbeler. — First edition.

pages cm

Summary: After bedtime a house comes alive as a lamp in the shape
of a bird solves an array of problems including a leaky faucet, a creaking
chair, and sneezing broom, all while the family sleeps.

ISBN 978-0-8234-3295-0 (hardcover)

 [1. Bedtime—Fiction. 2. Lamps—Fiction. 3. Noise—Fiction.] I. Title.

PZ7.E23Cl 2015

[E]—dc23

2014019244

Tip, tap, click, click.

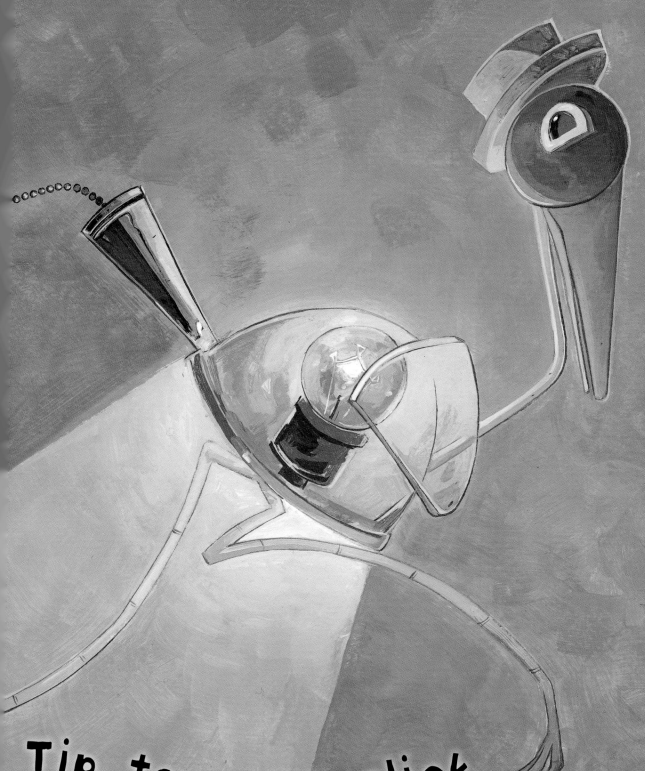

Tip, tap, click, click.

Rock, rock, creak, creak.

Tip, tap, click,

click. Tip, tap, click, click.

Swish, swish, glide, glide.

Slide, slide.

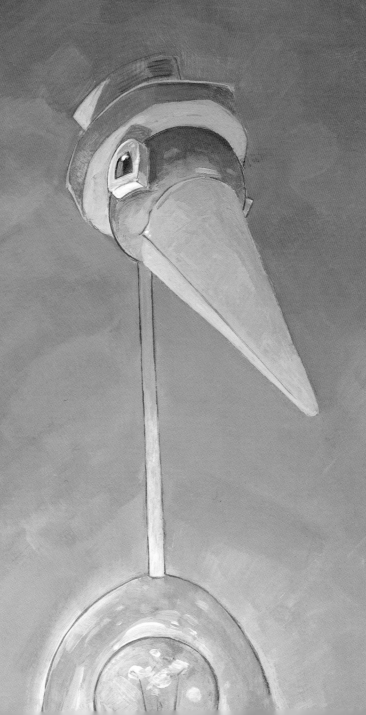

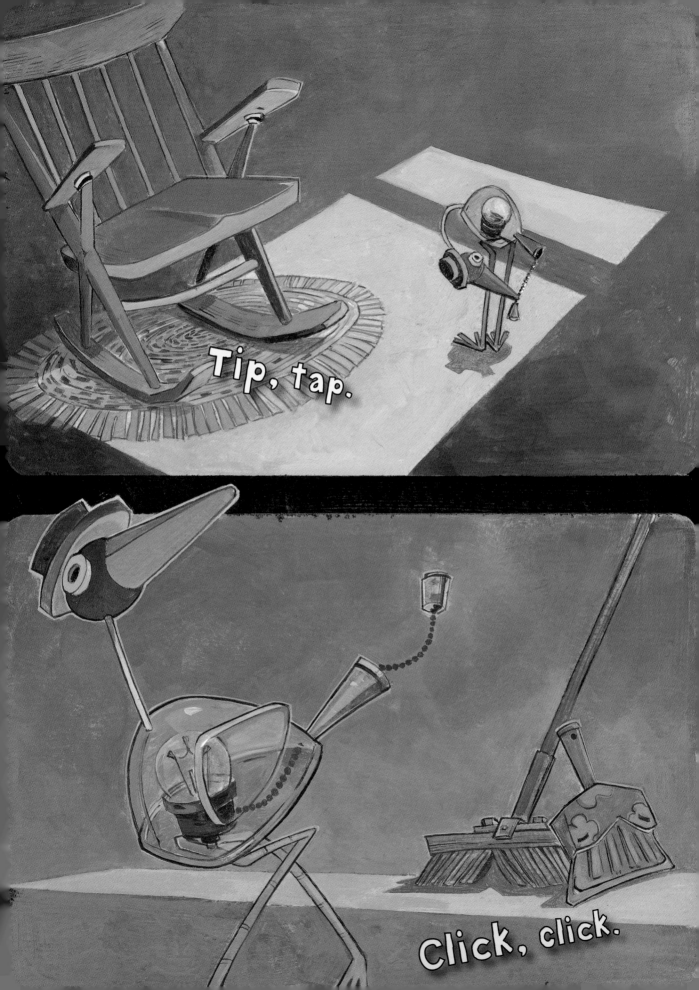

Tip, tap, click, click.

Nuzzle, nuzzle.

Click!